W9-BWJ-877

3 8538 00019 5789

E
SLAVIN, Bill
The cat came back

33077

STOCKTON
Township Public Library
Stockton, IL

Books may be drawn for two weeks and renewed once.

A fine of five cents a library day shall be paid for each
book kept overtime.

Borrower's card must be presented whenever a book is
taken. If card is lost a new one will be given for payment of
25 cents.

Each borrower must pay for damage to books.

KEEP YOUR CARD IN THIS POCKET

DEMCO

THE CAT CAME BACK

Library of Congress Cataloging-in-Publication Data
Slavin, Bill.
The cat came back/Bill Slavin.
p.   cm.
Summary: A persistent and indestructible cat
keeps coming back, despite his owner's attempts
to give him away.
ISBN 0-8075-1097-1
[1. Cats—Fiction. 2. Stories in rhyme.] *
I. Title.

PZ8.3.S63185Cat 1992   92-16382
[E]—dc20   CIP
                                                      AC

Illustrations © 1992 by Bill Slavin.
THE CAT CAME BACK is a trademark of
Oak Street Music Inc.
Published in 1992 by Albert Whitman & Company,
6340 Oakton, Morton Grove, Illinois 60053-2723.
Published by permission of Kids Can Press Ltd.,
Toronto, Ontario, Canada.
All rights reserved. No part of this publication
may be reproduced, stored in retrieval system, or
transmitted in any form or by any means, electronic,
mechanical photocopying, recording, or otherwise,
without the prior written permission of
Albert Whitman & Company.
Printed and bound in the U.S.A.
10   9   8   7   6   5   4   3   2   1

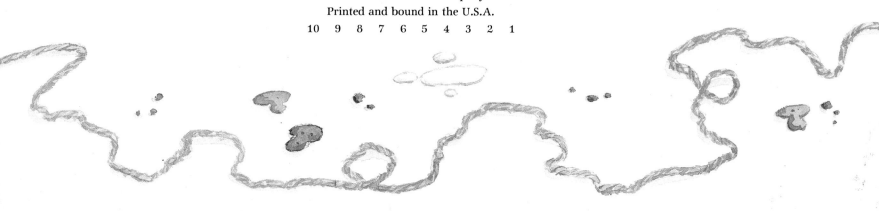

For my brother Jim,
who knows all the words.

THE CAT

A traditional song
illustrated by Bill Slavin

ALBERT WHITMAN & COMPANY
Morton Grove, Illinois

CAME BACK

Old Mister Johnson had
troubles of his own,
He had a yellow cat that
wouldn't leave his home.

He tried and he tried
to give that cat away,

He found an ocean liner going far, far away.

But the cat came back
    the very next day,
The cat came back,
    they thought he was a goner,
The cat came back,
    he just wouldn't stay away.

Mister Johnson gave the cat
to a man in a balloon,
He said, "Please take this cat
and leave it on the moon."

The balloon came down about
ninety miles away,
Where the man is now, well,
no one wants to say.

And the cat came back
   the very next day,
The cat came back,
   they thought he was a goner,
The cat came back,
   he just wouldn't stay away.

Mister Johnson gave the cat to a fellow heading west,

He said, "The cat's a present for the one you love the best."

First the train hit the track, then it bounced and jumped a rail,

Not a person stayed around to tell the gruesome tale.

And the cat came back
  the very next day,
The cat came back,
  they thought he was a goner,
The cat came back,
  he just wouldn't stay away.

The cat was now the father of a family of his own,
They lived with Mister Johnson 'til there came a cyclone.

It tore the house apart and tossed the cats around,
The air was filled with kittens,

the cat could not be found.

But the cat came back
the very next day,
The cat came back,
they thought he was a goner,
The cat came back,
he just wouldn't stay away.

THE CAT CAME BACK

Old Mis- ter John-son had trou- bles of his own, He

had a yel- low cat that would- n't leave his home. He

tried and he tried to give that cat a- way. He

found an o- cean lin- er go- ing far, far a- way. But the

cat came back the ver-y next day, The

cat came back, they thought he was a gon-er, The

cat came back, he just would-n't stay a-way.

Stockton Twp. Pub. Lib.
140 W. BENTON
STOCKTON, IL 61085